Pete the Cat and the Missing Cupcakes

Kimberly and James Dean

HARPER
An Imprint of HarperCollinsPublishers

MILK

To all of Pete's friends everywhere.
Matthew 6:14
—J.D. & K.D.

Pete the Cat and the Missing Cupcakes

For information address HarperCollins Children's Books, a division of HarperCollins Publishers,
195 Broadway, New York, NY 10007.
www.harpercollinschildrens.com

ISBN 978-0-06-230434-6 (trade bdg.)
ISBN 978-0-06-230435-3 (lib. bdg.)

The artist used pen and ink with watercolor and acrylic paint on
300lb press paper to create the illustrations for this book.
Typography by Jeanne L. Hogle
16 17 18 19 20 PC 10 9 8 7 6 5 4 3 2 1
❖
First Edition

Pete and Gus were as busy as could be.

They were getting ready for the cupcake party. It started at three!

They were making cupcakes for everyone.
Pete and Gus counted them just for fun!

They had ten when they were done.

OH NO! HANG ON!

Some of the cupcakes were gone!
They were sure there had been ten.

Pete said, "Maybe we need to count again!"

They counted the cupcakes
lined up straight.
Now there were only eight!

It looked like someone had taken two.

BUT WHO?

Pete and Gus did not know what to do!

Just then they found a clue.

Gus said, "Look what I have found. Sprinkles on the ground! I bet it was Squirrel. She loves sprinkles."

Squirrel said,

"It wasn't me!
It couldn't be!
I've been at the spelling bee!"

"Uh-oh. More cupcakes are missing. Come and see!"

THIS WAS TOO WEIRD!

Two more cupcakes
had disappeared!

Now there were only six!
Someone must be playing tricks!

BUT WHO?

Pete and Gus did not know what to do!

Just then they found
another clue!

Pete said, "I bet it was Alligator!
He loves to eat."

Alligator said,
"It wasn't me!
It couldn't be!
I've been learning my ABCs!"
"Uh-oh. More cupcakes
are missing. Come and see!"

Now there were only four!
Someone had taken two more!

BUT WHO?

Pete and Gus did not know what to do!
Just then they found another clue.

"I bet it was Turtle," said Pete.
"I know Turtle loves sweets."

Turtle said,

"It wasn't me!
It couldn't be!
I've been swimming in the sea!"

"Uh-oh. More cupcakes are missing.
Come and see!"

What on earth was going on?
All the cupcakes were now
GONE!

Pete and Gus did not know what to do!

They started looking for another clue.

They found Grumpy Toad with icing on his face!
Pete and Gus have solved the case.

"I am so sorry!
It WAS me!

I could not stop with just one!
I ate and ate 'til there were none!"

Everyone agreed—Grumpy Toad would have to miss the fun.

He could not come after what he had done.

Pete said, "But wait! Grumpy Toad made a mistake. This is true. Let's give him a second chance. That's what friends do!"

Pete told Grumpy Toad they would give him another chance.

He was so excited. He did a happy dance!

The night of the party was so much fun. Grumpy Toad brought more than enough cupcakes for everyone!

PETE the CAT'S
CUPCAKE PARTY

MEOW